T0063326

MASK

of

LEGEND

JOSEPH ALBERICI

abbott press

Abbott Press books may be ordered through booksellers or by contacting:

Abbott Press
1663 Liberty Drive
Bloomington, IN 47403
www.abbottpress.com
Phone: 1-866-697-5310

Because of the dynamic nature of the Internet, any web addresses or
links contained in this book may have changed since publication and
may no longer be valid. The views expressed in this work are solely those
of the author and do not necessarily reflect the views of the publisher,
and the publisher hereby disclaims any responsibility for them.

Any people depicted in stock imagery provided by Thinkstock are models,
and such images are being used for illustrative purposes only.
Certain stock imagery © Thinkstock.

ISBN: 978-1-4582-1829-2 (sc)
ISBN: 978-1-4582-1830-8 (e)

Library of Congress Control Number: 2014921793

Print information available on the last page.

Abbott Press rev. date: 04/30/2015

For my family who helped me greatly publishing this book.

Thanks especially to my father my mother my aunt Carissa for donating much money and my grandmother who got me my first few notebooks.

CONTENTS

PROLOGUE

Toronto Canada, 2006

"We need to ship it now so the next boat will take it to London. We need it there by next month" John yelled.

"The order needs to be shipped by two o'clock; we've got four hours." Bill giggled.

"Yes, but right now is the shipment with the diamond."

Bill spat the hot cup of coffee on the floor. "Oh! Let's get this shipment moving!"

Meanwhile

"No!" A 9 year old child with blonde hair tied up in a bun shrieked. "My mask, my mask it's my favorite one!" She also wore skinny jeans and flip flops with a t-shirt that was pink and white tidied.

The mask had been a gift from her ancestors. The ancestors of the child had created it with the purest of fabrics. It was a beautiful creation, but there was something special about this particular mask. No one could figure out if this was an accident or if someone meant for this mask to have such a great ability. It was sometimes a great thing but sometimes people thought as to lock it up. But the masked managed to be passed on throughout the family. It was always meant to be kept by a responsible person. If near the mask would make anything you would want reality. Sadly enough, the ability was forgotten for a long period of time until brought back by Lydia M. Abrahams, the child who had possession of it now.

"Lydia, we could always get you another one," her mother said.

"But you don't understand," Lydia screamed.

"Yes I do—you have an obsession with it."

"No, it makes my wishes come true."

"Stop telling fibs, Lydia. That's not how a young lady speaks."

The mask sifted into the crate down below which happens to be the crate John was about to ship, and that's how this story starts off.

CHAPTER 1

The Disappearance

"Ok that's everything, Bill," John said as he finished loading everything into the ship.

"You're good," Bill yelled out to the boat driver.

Oxford shire, London, 2009

"The shipment has finally arrived, after all these days," a local townsperson yelled. He opened the box. It was just as he expected, a 100% pure seven inch diamond crystal. "Hmm … what's this?" He saw the mask. "This won't sell for a dime," he tossed the mask into the street.

The mask sat there for at least 7 years. Days later a prisoner got out of jail and was walking down the street he saw the mask. In his eyes the mask was a treasure, not many other people could see the true potential in the mask. But a criminal liking the mask was a bad thing. Not only would good wishes become true but if one wishes to have someone put on the moon it would come true. He could not see the ability clearly but he knew it was something special.

"I wish that all the police would vanish, those fools, I wish they'd perish," the prisoner (Sebastian Woods) said repulsively. A week later the police had been reported missing.

Same time in North Yorkshire

"The newspaper is finally here, Lydia."

"I'll be there in a second, mother."

"Well, this is surprising…"

"What is it? H-how could I forget? The mask… it's it has fallen into the wrong hands."

"Remember what I said about that stupid mask! I cannot stand it anymore. If you even start thinking about that stupid mask again you don't even want to know what I'm going to do," Lydia's mother screamed.

"I've got to go somewhere."

"Come back in two hours, or you're grounded!"

"No promises."

"Where are you going? Answer me!"

"Back to London. You'll see me again in a couple of weeks."

"Lydia Abrahams, come back here right now!"

Then Emma darted off into the street, she kept on running. I've got to go to the express plane in time or I won't be able to get to London before something bad happens, but the airport that holds the express plane is over 2 miles away, she thought.

I'm never going to make it in time it leaves in two minutes! I have, got, to, hurry! She passed a sign that read, "Toronto express airport 0.2 miles away. *Oh no!* she thought, *I've only got 1 minute left before the plane leaves.* She ran so fast things were blurring different colors as she sprinted furiously through the street.

There, the airport, only twenty feet away! 10, she ripped the door open with tremendous strength.

9, she ran so fast through the crowded airport she felt like she was going to have a heart attack. She flew past the metal detectors strangely no people were guarding them in case of hidden guns. "Ah, excuse me miss." A shady figure smiled "which plane might you be taking?"

"The plane that's leaving in 6…"

"I do not mean to be rude by proving you wrong, young miss, but I believe that plane has been delayed, it leaves in thirty minutes". He pointed his outstretched arm to the plane departure chart. It read, Plane 73 leaving in 30 minutes.

"Oh, well then, I guess it does." Emma looked around, everyone was staring at her. "Thank you for the advice sir, um by the way I didn't happen to catch your name."

"My name is Samuel Haden, and yours?"

"Lydia Abrahams, it is a pleasure to meet you."

"Yes, you too. So, what's the reason you need to ride this plane?"

"I'm checking out disappearances of police officers in Oxford Shire," Lydia exclaimed.

"Strange I'm going there for the same reason. Did you hear the news about the incident at London's finest restaurant?"

"No, but what happened?"

"A prisoner made the perfect crime. He stole more than half the food! He smashed all the video cameras and sprayed poisonous gas to knock out the chefs, manager, patrons and waitresses and waiters! It is simply miraculous that he thought of everything in about five hours!"

"In five hours, but that seems almost impossible!"

"Yes, the article in the paper I read said that the criminal had been out of jail for five hours then commits a crime like that!"

"I see he must be a very smart person." God, that mask is really going to get someone hurt if I don't make it to London in time, Lydia thought. She looked around cautiously then started walking to a chair. Everyone seemed frightened of her.

"The plane to London has just arrived we will be taking off in 20 minutes," the intercom lady moaned. It seemed as if she really hated her job.

A couple minutes passed. Lydia tried everything to enjoy the spare time. Then she thought; *what if my mother comes here soon!* As if on cue her mother barged into the room with a terribly angry face.

"We now are ready to board fliers," the lady announced.

"Samuel we have to hurry and get on. My mother is right there," Lydia pointed.

"Well, I guess it's time to go," Samuel said hurriedly.

But they didn't know what awaited them on this particular express plane.

CHAPTER 2

The Express Plane

Lydia and Samuel entered the plane just before Lydia's mother snatched her. The next plane for Oxford Shire was in a week so they were good for a while. It was a very luxurious plane. It had many chairs where a massage machine was built in. The plane was of great length.

"Ticket, miss, you do need a ticket—you know that right?" the ticket receiver groaned.

"Um, yes, very sorry."

"I have," Samuel looked at her name tag. "I have two, Miss Chelsea. One must always have two in case of an emergency," Samuel said.

"Thank you very much," Lydia yelled.

"Excuse me miss but no yelling on this plane, people have paid a very high price, I believe they would want this to be a relaxing trip, thank you," the ticket receiver hissed.

"Hmm, it seems like every person that's working here is miserable, tired, and really, really depressed," Lydia whispered.

"Yes, that's true, but never mind that, let's find our seats," Samuel said.

They walked down the plane for about thirty seconds until they found their seats. J2 and J3 were their seats. Luckily their seats had the massage machines built in to it. Samuel and Emma turned them on.

"Wow this machine is fantastic, really, I can't believe it!" Lydia turned the dial up, her eyes got heavy.

"Hmm, you are right this machine feels amazing!"

Lydia looked over to the seat across the walkway. The people sitting there were wearing tinted glasses, black suits raised up to their noses. They also wore boots and gloves. They were both about six feet tall. Next to them were two black and silver briefcases. They looked very mysterious.

"I wonder what's in the briefcases," Lydia yawned.

"The plane should be leaving in approximately two minutes," the intercom lady groaned.

"Well we better sit back and relax before this plane takes off, get buckled," Samuel demanded.

"Alright, well here we go," Lydia exclaimed.

It was then completely silent. "We are now taking off." The plane made a gurgling sound then took flight. About ten minutes passed then a waitress came out with refreshments, "Would you like anything sir?"

"No, would you Lydia."

"Yes I'd like a glass of water."

"Here you go miss," the waitress handed over the water with ease. "Would you like anything else," the waitress asked.

"No I'm settled for now, thank you though," replied Lydia. The waitress smiled and continued down the walkway.

"Well she wasn't so grumpy like the other ladies," Samuel grinned. She stopped and asked the next person.

"Would..." Bam! The mysterious people with the black suits shot a gun at one of the glasses. "AHH" the waitress screamed.

One of the mysterious people stood up and pushed the woman to the ground then raised his gun up in the air and started shooting. Everyone in the plane was afraid.

"How could they possibly get passed the metal detectors if they had guns," Lydia asked.

"That's probably why the guards weren't there," Samuel exasperated. Samuel rushed over to the bruised lady on the floor behind him. "Are you alright Miss?" Samuel questioned.

"Yes, it's just minor bruises and a few cuts from the glass." Samuel walked up to the robbers and punched both of them right in the face. But then one of the robbers came back with a sickly punch to Samuel's face. Then Samuel tried to kick them in their shins but they jumped aside.

"Who are you?" Samuel questioned.

"We are world class criminals, were wanted in almost all of North America," one hissed.

"Yes, but what are your identifications?"

"It wouldn't matter, there fake," the other sneered. One pulled out his gun. Samuel kicked him in his stomach. He flew towards the end of the plane. Samuel walked over to him.

"I have had enough of you," the criminal said menacingly. He shot the gun, Samuel dodged it. It hit Samuel's massage machine, the machine blew up and knocked Lydia to her knees, Lydia screamed.

"Are you alright Lydia," Samuel asked.

"Yes I'm alright," Lydia said fearfully. Samuel kneed the robber in his chest then smacked the gun out of his hand. The other robber snuck up behind Samuel. The other robber went to kick him but Samuel caught his leg and tossed him into the wall. Samuel smashed the robber's skulls into the walls. One of the robbers tried to pick up his gun. Samuel stepped on his fingers then picked up the gun. Samuel smacked both of them with the gun. They went to chase him but Samuel walked away, he knew it was over. They both fell down, knocked out cold. Samuel went to walk back to his seat.

Everyone was thanking him. Even the groaning, exhausted lady that had the cuts and bruises thanked him. He walked over to Lydia, her chair was in flames. Samuel yanked the fire extinguisher out of the wall and sprayed it all over the chair. The fire was put out. The waitresses came over to Samuel with a bottle of Champagne.

"Here you go sir, our complements" the bruised lady smiled. "Would you like to move to a different seat Miss Emma"?

"Yes, I would".

"Unfortunately, the only available seats are the ones that the criminals were sitting at, are you still interested?"

"I'll take it, it'll probably be better than this one" Emma said. She looked around the seat was totally destroyed. She limped across the walkway, her leg must've been hurt from the massage machine blowing up. They looked over at the end of the plane. There were the two criminals that had robbed every state in all most all of North America.

"We'll were should we keep them until we arrive at London? There are no police on board" one person asked another.

"I bet most people wouldn't care if we threw them off board" the other one said.

"Yeah, I bet they wouldn't mind it, but we don't have the custody to throw them off the plane" the first one responded.

"I guess we could just lock them up in the storage closet".

"Well I guess so" the first one decided.

"Then that's what we'll do". They slowly dragged them both behind through the walkway and then opened the staff doors.

"What the..." one of the thugs woke up. BAM! The staff hit him on his head then threw him into the closet, same with the other. "Well that better keep them still for a while" laughed the one that had hit the robber. Everything was back to normal on the plane. Emma peered out her window the plane was moving incredibly fast. The clouds were blurring past. It was now about mid afternoon she had spent about an hour and a half on the plane.

She sat back this seat didn't have the massage machine. Wow world class robbers and they couldn't afford a massage seat, Lydia thought. She looked around everyone seemed satisfied. The intercom was active.

"We should be arriving in London in approximately ten hours."

"Wow this plane is very astonishingly fast, usually this trip would take over a whole day on a normal plane," Samuel barked.

"Open the door!" The robber yelled. They started to pound on the door. But they knew they would not be getting out very soon.

"I hope there are not going to be very many more incidents, because that one hurt a little" Samuel complained. Samuel took the bottle of Champagne and poured a small bubbling glass of it. It tasted very refreshing. Samuel looked across the walkway.

Emma had fallen into a deep sleep. Sooner or later he fell asleep too. After all he had been through a lot, he deserved a small rest. He woke up all the tension in his muscles were relieved. He looked across the walkway again, Emma was still asleep. A couple of minutes passed, the intercom came on again.

"We should be arriving shortly, at most three hours" the lady said more cheerfully this time.

Samuel wondered if it was because he defeated the robbers or if it was because the ride was almost over. He was hoping the second one because if so they'd be in a better mood for the last three hours of the ride.

"Buzz" something sounded "Buzz" it rang again. Samuel looked around to see were it was coming from. The sound was quite annoying. "Buzz" Lydia finally woke up. She took her cell phone out of her pocket. That was what the buzzing noise was. She answered it. The voice that came out was extremely mad and loud.

"LYDIA ABRAHAMS, WHERE ARE YOU"! Her mother screamed enraged.

"I-I'm a-at the library".

"FOR THIRTEEN HOURS"! Her mother screamed still full of rage and fury.

"I've got to go, bye."

"LYD-" her mother was cut off. She hung up, after that she silenced her phone. She wouldn't want to be yelled at again to be quiet. Most of the people were sleeping. Ckkkk, the newly appearing lightning outside was rumbling. Ckkkk, it started to grow a little louder. CKKKK, it was now extremely loud. The raindrops outside were pouring down in globs. CKKKK, BOOM, the lightning had hit a propeller. The intercom came on again.

"Please put on your breathing masks" the lady exclaimed. But everyone was sleeping besides himself and Lydia.

"Lydia, you've got to help me wake everyone up before the plane crashes" yelled Samuel.

"Alright I'll hurry" Lydia claimed. Samuel and Emma went around waking everyone up and telling them to put on their breathing masks. Most of them woke up easily, a couple needed a few shakes. They all had their breathing masks on now.

"If everyone could please put on their seatbelts and sit down that would be much appreciated" the lady said anxiously.

The plane started to fly downwards, everyone was screaming. Samuel went to the back, it seemed like he was going to be able to fix it! The intercom came on.

"Sir I wouldn't advise to try to fix it we've only got about forty seconds till we crash."

"Do you have any spare parts for an engine?" Samuel asked.

"Well we have two left over combustion chambers and a spare radiator input hose," responded the intercom lady.

"Great, one of the combustion chambers got fried which made the radiator input hose get electrocuted! Let me see just…"

"Excuse me sir we have thirteen seconds till we crash," the lady on the intercom said anxiously.

"There, all I need is a spring…" Samuel looked at the airplane attendance. "Does anyone happen to have a spring," Samuel asked.

"I have one no, I have two, one of the ladies in the crowd yelled. There for my pens, here have them," she smiled.

"That won't fit, but it will reduce the amount of damage this plane takes," Samuel insisted.

"Three seconds," the lady sat out quickly.

"Just slip these on, and there." Samuel hopped back into his seat. The airport came into view. They weren't quite going to make it. "Strap on tight Lydia, this plane is going to crash," Samuel requested.

It was all up to Samuel's genius now. The pressure was pounding on Samuel's heart. Everyone's lives were in Samuel's hands now. A jolt was felt. Then a shake, then a feeling of your insides being turned out, it was horrible. The experience was mind shattering, the loud noises of metal versus concrete. But concrete won, it was now over. Everyone's minds were fluttering with emotions of hope, depression, fear and joyfulness.

Samuel opened his eyes. None were dead, but most unconscious. Oh, no the captain and the waitress, Samuel thought. He opened the captain doors. The captain was, gone. Glass had scythed his eyes, nose and forehead. But the waitress was still alive. Bleeding harshly, but alive.

Samuel himself was injured; his leg had been bruised very badly. He struggled to limp back to his seat, he couldn't take the pain he slouched over and fell. His skull was bleeding, his leg was bruised and two of his ribs had snapped. He peered up. Lydia had awoken. Her right leg jammed between the seats in front of her and her own. The door to the plane opened. Two officers and two doctors came in.

"Everyone are, you all, alright," they yelled. At least four people answered. They all wheezed yes. We are taking you all to the hospital. At long last the trip was over, no more fights or storms. But the hospital and London itself might be worse than the plane trip. The roaring sound of ambulances arrived. Then squad cars and fire trucks, only five minutes had passed and it seemed a state worth attendance were there. Two doctors had picked Samuel up and heaved him up on a stretcher. But something didn't seem right. His mind went blank and he blacked out. The last thing he heard was people screaming.

CHAPTER 3

London

When Samuel woke up two hours later he was then in a hospital. "Let me out, where's Lydia she has to call her mother."

"Ah, the girl she is over there with the people closest to her name, that's how we sort things here. She lays unconscious next to Lloyd and Lynus, the criminals of the plane. They were located in a cloth closet," she responded.

"Let her call her mother when she wakes up, please," Samuel pleaded. The nurse walked away. "Please," Samuel called out.

Lydia's eyes fluttered. The same nurse that had tended to Samuel was hulking over her with a cell phone reaching out.

"A man insisted that you call your mother."

"Alright," Lydia said weakly. Hand me the phone." She took the phone struggling to raise her hand. She pressed the cubed numbers. After she stopped a buzzing sound was heard. Someone picked up.

"Hey, mom," she sobbed.

"Lydia! Please, tell me, where are you," Her mom asked.

"I-I'm in London."

"Please come back I beg of you."

"I can't I don't have enough money to come home." Tears were now streaming down her face.

"I'll ride over and pick you up."

"No, mom please, don't I have to obtain the mask."

"AGAIN, the freaking mask I've had enough of this!"

"Mom, I have to go." Lydia then hung up. "It's always useless trying to call my mom." The lady came back.

"Can I help you to anything?"

"Yes actually, can you escort me to breakfast?"

"Yes, just hop out of bed and we'll be on our way," the nurse smiled. She got out of bed and realized many of the people riding the plane were in the same room she was in. None of the people had as bad injuries as Samuel. As she was exiting the room she then saw that he wasn't there.

"Excuse me, but were did my friend Samuel get put," Lydia asked.

"Oh, Samuel Haden, he is in intensive treatment, he had gotten seriously injured," the nurse said warily.

"Can I visit him before we go to the breakfast room," Lydia questioned.

"I'm sorry but he needs rest before anyone can see him," the nurse replied.

"Alright, excuse me but what would your name happen to be," Lydia asked.

"My name is nurse Sienna, now Miss Lydia we should go to breakfast," Sienna smiled.

As Emma limped through the hallways she recognized people she met a long time ago when she used to live in London. Not very many, but she did, there was Mr. Smith the cheery optimist that lived in there street. There was also Ms. Cory Norman. She used to be the neighborhood grump. Last but not least, (that would've been Ms. Norman) there was Mr. Red he was an electrical supplies man. He was always friendly like Mr. Smith, they reached the breakfast room.

A wonderful aroma infiltrated Emma's nose as she walked inside. They served the biggest selection of food Emma had ever seen in her life. There were sausages, fruits, cereals, even milkshakes. The food was really great too. She enjoyed her delectable meals as she watched television on a fifty-two inch flat screen TV. The hospital was fantastic almost too fantastic. The delicious sausage filled her mouth with taste and flavor as she ravenously wolfed down more and more.

But unfortunately, soon enough she got full and the meal was over. She stood up and felt like she gained twenty pounds, and she probably did eating five to ten sausages and at least seven biscuits which were amazing and had glorious flavor. She limped over to the exit. Her leg still injured badly. She started to walk back over to the room she had come from when a message popped up on the TV. She looked at it.

"Hello this Zachary Morrow and I'm am here to tell you about the incident at express plane port seven. A plane had crashed leaving serious injuries on most passengers. Lucky for them brave Samuel Haden had fixed the engine that had gotten struck by lightning just enough so that no one would get killed in the monstrous inferno of spiraling death. But in that act of bravery, he was put in intensive treatment at the biggest hospital in town the La` Carpriunco. Now here's Casey Dean with the weather," Morrow smiled.

She felt amazed that Samuel was a hero yet also her friend. She had arrived at her room and lay back down in her bed. Samuel grabbed a pair of crutches and hopped out of bed. His body ached all over. The pain was tremendous as he took one step, and then two. He did not care for breakfast his only means were to get some fresh air in the park right outside the building. Luckily for him the doctor knocked on the door.

"Excuse me sir, it's time for you to go outside if you'd like," the doctor smiled.

"Definitely, thank you." Samuel got up painfully. He opened the door of his room and travelled down the hallways until they reached the main doors that led to exit. He started to open the main doors, the fresh air felt comforting against his sore aching body.

He sat down on a bench in front of the building and laid down his crutches. London was beautiful, there were smooth colored leaves falling gently from many tree's dark branches. Bicyclers rode and waved at cars passing throughout the black topped streets. A cool breeze seemed to flow with birds flying happily high up in the unpolluted sky. Samuel paused, his complicated mind relaxed and then, then he smiled, he enjoyed the sight, squirrels nibbling on acorns and people walking mannered dogs. He became drowsy it felt like this was all too good. He lay back on the bench. Swiftly and soon he fell asleep, into a deep sleep. When he woke up he was back in bed in his room, they must've taken him in when he was sleeping outside on the bench.

He made no effort to ask for more time outside because it would only cause pain now that he was satisfied. The week went on slowly, after four days Lydia was healed and ready to get out of what was seemed a jail, but as for Samuel, he wasn't going to get out for another five weeks. Slowly but surely he was getting better. After two weeks of waiting he needed to escape, he couldn't take walking around the same exact place for more than a month. If he escaped it wouldn't be long before another hospital caught him wheezing in pain. He was pretty much trapped at what this seemed as a torture chamber more than of a hospital.

Two Weeks Later

After a long time of waiting, and sleeping Samuel was aloud out of the hospital. He was grateful. Feeling perfectly fine he made his way out of the dreaded hospital. He looked around, and no I'm not going to give the nice peaceful vision again there's no more nice stuff. Samuel waited until Emma came for her normal daily check up. Hours passed and when she came Samuel gave her the good news. They went to a local research facility. Luckily everyone there knew Samuel because of his spontaneous rescues around the world. After long nights of researching and investigating the town they had come to a conclusion.

After all the dreaded, slow, harsh sleepless nights of research they came to a mind blowing result. The one who obtained this horrible mask of life and death was none other than Sebastian Woods, the prisoner who got released performed a perfect crime leaving no trace, then got swept off of everyone's minds. "I should've known, all this time I didn't have the slightest idea. Err, someone's been playing mind games," Samuel smiled. He rushed out of the facility and started to ask around and everyone gave him puzzled looks like he was stupid. But then he asked a child.

"Why, Sir, don't you know he's the prime minister?"

Samuel stared in horror. "No, that's insane," Samuel cried.

CHAPTER 4

Sebastian Woods Prime Minister

"When will we start attempting to attack," Lydia asked.

"Oh, I've already done that, we're attacking tonight," Samuel grinned.

"Tonight, we're not prepared at all," Lydia screamed.

"Maybe you're not but I am," Samuel responded.

"It's only been three weeks," Lydia cried.

Samuel and Emma made their way to the greatest building in all of London. That's where the prime minister lives, currently Sebastian Woods.

"He has many guards there, it will be very difficult to get in," Samuel exclaimed.

"I can't believe we're attacking only after three weeks of looking at this situation," Lydia pouted.

"I've drawn diagrams of this building inside and out and I've figured out the best way to get to his room," Samuel explained. "Unfortunately we will have to climb into the air vents in a certain part."

"The air vents, nasty," Lydia screamed.

"Alright are you ready, Lydia," Samuel asked.

"Yes, but I don't want to," Lydia complained.

"We will start by entering formal. Next if everything goes well we will enter the left path, when we near his door that when the air vents come in," Samuel grinned.

They opened the door, a group of people touring the building. They fit in just right in with them.

"We weren't scheduled though, this is bad," Lydia complained.

"Nope I've scheduled," Samuel said. He pulled two tickets out of one of his pockets. They were orange and real, they would get them in. The group travelled to the ticket master. He eyed Lydia and Samuel suspiciously.

"I've never seen you two before and I know nearly everyone," the ticket master claimed. "Wait you guys look familiar, do I know you." As the ticket master talked to himself, he looked at their tickets and allowed them to move on. About an hour later they came to the left and right paths.

"This is where we depart, Samuel barked. They slyly walked to the left path unnoticed by the tourist group travelling down the right path. They walked past many rare artifacts and many unreal things. As they continued walking down the path they spotted guards and guards spotted them.

"Hey you're not supposed to be down here," one of the five guards yelled. They all began fighting, it was a mad house. As Lydia fought them all at once Samuel took them out one by one by covering there noses and mouths. Soon enough all of the guards were knocked out. The air vent was only a few feet away. Samuel unscrewed it and climbed in then he pulled Lydia up. They travelled slowly through the air vents as it was extremely hard to navigate.

Sooner or later they came to a halt. There it was the prime ministers bedroom. As Emma and

Samuel looked around at the room from the vents they came to a discovery. No one was in there, so they waited and waited and waited. Soon enough they grew tired and started to fall asleep. Samuel woke up to a sudden creak of the door. A figure walked in, it must've been Sebastian Woods. Three others walked next to him, two elite guards and his prime butler.

Samuel shook Lydia, she woke up. "He's here, but not only him but guards and a butler," Samuel explained.

"Well if the guards fighting skills are as good as the ones we fought before it won't be much of a problem," Lydia yawned.

"There elites so they'll be tougher," Samuel claimed. "But the real problem is Sebastian Woods, I don't know how tough he will be, let alone with the mask," Samuel whispered.

"Wait you know about the mask," Lydia yelled.

"Huh, what was that" Sebastian Woods yelled. They all looked around eying every nook and cranny.

"Quiet, yes I know about the mask and I'll tell you how later but for now we have to act fast," Samuel barked.

"Who is that, this is the prime minister and you better show yourself or else," Sebastian roared.

"Check the air vents sir," the butler suggested. Sebastian hopped into the vents with unnatural powers into the vents and wormed his way through them. When he caught up to them they were right at the exit of the vents. Unfortunately Sebastian caught Samuel's leg, it was over Samuel was being dragged back to the room.

"No, Lydia, leave I'll be fine," Samuel exclaimed.

"You don't know what you've gotten yourself into," Sebastian grinned.

"Stop this, let him go," Lydia sobbed.

"Lydia what did I say, go hurry before it's too late," Samuel yelled.

Sebastian smirked and they were gone, disappeared, vanished into thin air.

"No, this can't be," Lydia cried. She crawled out of the vents moaning.

Wham! Samuel hit ground hard, he looked around he was back at the prime minister or Sebastian's bedroom. Before Samuel's mind came back to him a defeating punch landed in his stomach. He bent down and a gruesome knee smashed his skull. Samuel blinked Sebastian was right in front of him. He kicked him in his chest and Samuel was practically tossed across the room. Blood was now slowly coming out of his mouth.

Samuel tried to fight back but he had an unforgiving concussion and he couldn't focus. Sebastian head butted Samuel in the forehead. Stunned, Samuel could barely open his eyes. All he could see was fist and foot. Sebastian had already clearly defeated Samuel but he wasn't letting this go. Samuel now devastatingly beat up was picked up by his neck.

"You don't know the world of pain you've gotten yourself into, this is just the beginning." Sebastian laughed and tossed Samuel into the wall. "I've heard you know a little something about this," Sebastian claimed. He pulled an object out of one of his pockets. It was the mask, the long awaited mask of legend. Samuel stared at it and looked up at Sebastian with a painful bloody smile.

"Yes I know a little something about it," Samuel coughed.

"Tell me, is this magic," Sebastian asked.

"Why should I tell you," Samuel questioned.

"Because death is already knocking at your door," Sebastian grinned. He kicked Samuel in his chest. He coughed up blood, Samuel couldn't move.

"No I will not tell you," Samuel wheezed.

"I've killed men for questioning me and I've killed men for telling me no, which one should I kill you for," Sebastian growled.

"Neither, grr," Samuel screamed. The fight was again on. Samuel tried to punch and when it landed it hurt Samuel. His knuckles were bruised badly, now even worse.

"You can't beat me," Sebastian laughed. Samuel summoned all his strength or whatever he had left of it. Then he charged at Sebastian or the prime minister. When he hit Sebastian the air came out of his lungs. Sebastian only stuttered back a little bit.

Samuel grabbed one of Sebastian's body guards. Sebastian pounded him by accident. Samuel tossed him to the floor, then dodged a punch that would decimated him. But Sebastian still grabbed his arm and punched Samuel in the gut. Sebastian nailed him in his face. Then Sebastian released an ear deafening squeal. His muscles grew and the room cracked around him. His eyes flashed white and red. He had a devilish look on his face. He punched the wall and his arm sunk in it. Most of his body guards ran out of the room terrified.

"Wow, hose are some loyal body guards you have," Samuel chuckled.

"This is no time to be making jokes. I'm going to kill you."

"Well you haven't even managed to knock me out yet."

"You're pushing it," Sebastian spit in is face "Pal."

Samuel leaped backwards and dodged the flurry of attacks coming towards him. He jumped off of the floor and went to strike Sebastian. But

Sebastian blocked, and then Samuels's foot smashed into his face.

"You're an excellent fighter, you know," Sebastian grinned "But I have other things on my side."

"Like WHAT," Samuel screamed and lunged yet again. But Sebastian counter-attacked.

"Well for one, out of the many, this mask!" He yelled. He wailed and a blast of white energy radiated out of his mouth. It his Samuel and he bashed into a wall. Samuel was down for the count.

"Good night," Sebastian cackled.

His arm turned to cement and smashed into Samuels face. The sound of his own bones cracking rattled in his ears. He was knocked out cold. He thought he'd be back in s hospital for sure. His whole body was numb, it was the end his only hope was Lydia.

CHAPTER 5

Lydia's Time

Lydia is now Samuel's only hope. Being tormented in the palace of the Prime Minister, Lydia must come soon because Samuel is near death. Now starting to wake up, Sebastian had to deal with Samuel.

"Ha, you're not getting out of this alive," Sebastian chortled. He made a face liked he was making the last punt in a soccer game and kicked Samuel across the room. "Take him away," Sebastian commanded.

The one elite guard picked Samuel up by his wrists and dragged him out. People stared at Samuel like he wasn't human. He knew he was scratched up bad. As they passed by the ticket master he shouted something but Samuel couldn't hear it his head was spinning so badly.

"That's who you are, you're the man who saved all the people on the plane," the ticket master yelled with glee. As soon as he noticed that Samuel was badly injured he asked what happened.

"Oh, just another spy or something," the elite guard smiled.

"Oh so you know," the ticket master chuckled. Samuel did not know what was going on. Lydia looked around the vents took her outside near some dumpsters. She heard the clang and creaking of the palace's front door opening and sudden blood curdling yell. She raced to the front of the palace. Out of the corner of eye she saw Samuel and the two guards.

"Oh, my god, what've they done to him," Lydia cried. She raced over to them but she knew she couldn't make it. They two guards were taking him to a car about fifty yards from where they were currently standing. Lydia was standing about two hundred yards from the car. Still she panicked and raced to the car but knew she could never make it in time.

Samuel's head slowly turned, weakly and franticly. She ran faster than ever, two times faster than when she travelled to the plane. Still she was not quick enough. Samuel caught a glimpse of her with his eye. They approached the car ten feet away but Lydia was still at least seventy-five yards away. She continued running. One of the guards popped open one of the doors and tossed Samuel in.

"No," Lydia screamed. The guards hopped in. Tears started running down Lydia's eyes. The car came alive, but she was so close now. The car was put into reverse, backed up and cranked into drive. Lydia had no idea what to do, so she leaped. She took a great leap of faith, and, she made it. She hung on by her hands and her feet dragged behind her. She pulled herself up until she was in a crouching position. Then she hoisted herself to the roof. She scooted up on the roof until she got to the main glass. She kicked the glass in between her and the guards. It cracked, she hit again and again and again.

"What the crap," one of the guards yelled. They swerved, stopped suddenly and did every thing possible to swerve Lydia off. But Lydia would not give up that easily. She kicked and kicked and, CKKKKKKKKK. The glass shattered, the guards were showered with glass.

"Ah," the guards screamed in unison. The car was near it's destination to, the state penitentiary. The car rammed into tree's and caught on fire. She knew she had a matter of seconds to get Samuel out. She crawled down as fast as she could. To her surprise the car was unlocked. She opened a door and dragged Samuel out.

He hollered in excruciating pain, she didn't realize how bad his injuries were. They limped towards a safe distance. They did not travel far enough. It was now exploding in five seconds. They limped as fast as they could but they weren't fast enough. Samuel gather maximum strength for his current state and covered Lydia's head with his hand and jumped away from the detonating car. They dove and landed.

"Ahhhh," Samuel hollered. Lydia looked back. One of the guards struggled to get out. The other must've been knocked out. The active guard plopped onto the ground. He smiled that it hadn't blown up yet. As soon as he got up and looked around… BOOOOOOOOOOOOOOOOOOOOOOOOM! The car exploded, little pieces of leather, and metal were flying around. The explosion charred Samuel's face. As well as Lydia's face.

Well, the guards didn't really make it to a safe spot. Lydia and Samuel were pretty much breathing them. Lydia got up while Samuel was unconscious on the ground. She looked around warily. Her entire body and all limbs felt like jelly. One of the guards had been burned, charred and most of his remains were in a tree. The other must've been completely incinerated because there was no sign of him ever being there, at least outside of the car.

Lydia limped to the car, and unfortunately there he was. Or at least what was left of him. Lydia limped back over to Samuel and fell down. She looked up and Sebastian was there. She tried to get up but she was too weak then she went unconscious.

CHAPTER 6

The Ultimate Battle

Samuel and Emma woke up and looked around. They were in a strange place.

"Ah, I've seen you've awakened," Sebastian roared.

"Where, are we? This isn't Earth is it," Samuel said weakly.

"No, this is the moon, haven't you always wanted to go to the moon, because I have. Not much here though, rocks, stations and some dunes," Sebastian explained.

"Take us back to Earth, now," Samuel yelled.

"Well, you were climbing through my vents trying to burn my mask," Sebastian claimed.

"You used it for evil," Samuel mumbled.

"True but why not, I can do what ever now. I've been spying on you since you got to London. You are one of the only people that know I was ever a prisoner. Oh, and yes I have been playing mind games," Sebastian laughed.

Samuel got up he knew right know he had the advantage. He ran up to Sebastian but was no match for him. Sebastian's reflexes were amazing, he dodged, flipped, jumped, slid, and dove out of the way whenever Samuel went in for a punch. Lydia got up to she saw Samuel needed much help. She tried some different techniques but they knew they were no match for Sebastian's. They had been annihilated by Sebastian but weren't giving up. They punched, elbow, kicked, kneed, and even head butted but nothing hit.

They knew they were out matched. Sebastian could now just mutter something under his breath and his arms would become sandstone. Samuel wiped the slow dripping blood from his mouth. Then continued to battle, he tried everything but Sebastian out matched him. He slid up close to Sebastian to try and get a flurry of kicks and punches. As he went in Lydia sat up painfully. She saw him giving it all he had so she tried one last time.

Samuel missed every time he punched or kicked. He saw Lydia coming in quietly and understood. He tried to keep his attention off Lydia but Sebastian knew she was there. She played her trump card but before her punch even landed Sebastian's arm rocketed backwards and close lined her. She was down again. It was all up to Samuel now.

"You are only pests to me. I don't even need the mask to defeat you, ha, ha, ha," Sebastian roared in laughter. Lydia's eyes fluttered, she got back up. Sebastian came over to her before she was even standing on two feet. "Oh, how good, so you decided to join the party, well it's too late," Sebastian barked.

He kicked her head. She flew, blood streaming down her nose and mouth. Samuel was about ten feet away looking in horror.

"Do you always pick on the youth first?" Sebastian looked back over his shoulder.

"Don't worry I'll deal with you next," Sebastian smiled with pride. He scrambled over to what looked like Lydia's final resting spot. He picked her up by her head. His fist seemed to glow. He punched as hard as he could. She went sailing, farther than Samuel or Sebastian could see. Lydia was nearly dead. Her back must've broken from her landing. The moon was unforgiving.

"How sad, the poor girl's back is broken," Sebastian chuckled evilly.

"You monster," Samuel yelled.

"Me a monster, most people consider me as an inmate but that'll do fine," Sebastian exclaimed. He snapped his fingers a warm glow appeared. Lydia's back was fixed instantly. It was a miracle, now both Samuel and Sebastian understood the true power of the mask. Samuel rushed at Sebastian, using most of his strength he punched, Sebastian took the punch dead on grinned, and then swatted Samuel like a bug. Samuel crashed into a dune.

"You aren't thrilling in your current state," Sebastian frowned. He healed Samuel completely,

"Now that you're feeling well I suggest we continue our fight," Sebastian said calmly.

Samuel hopped out of the dune with more courage, bravery, and fight in him than ever. He fought Sebastian again. Samuel punched, kicked, dodged, and planned. Lydia stood up, scratched up bad, she was mad. Infuriated that Sebastian would heal her friend to continue torturing him. She ran up using all her energy to defeat her enemy who is Sebastian. She was coming in for the hit, she punched. Her eyes closed, when she opened them Sebastian was nowhere in sight. She backed up and bumped into someone.

Scared and fearful she looked behind her, luckily it was Samuel. She saw him planning. Trying to figure out where he'd gone. But Samuel couldn't figure it out he was just, gone. Vanished, like in the vents.

"Cowering again are you, Sebastian," Samuel yelled. A weird sonic sound came from behind Samuel. He looked behind him. There was Sebastian.

"You don't know the half of it," Sebastian cackled. "Yah," Sebastian screamed. A whirl of power came out of him. It was intense. "Gah," Sebastian screamed. "You think I'm a coward do you, well taste this, ya!" Sebastian sneered. A rocket of power came towards Samuel. He tried to leap out of the way but he was too late. It struck him, he crashed to the ground.

"No, Samuel," cried Lydia. Samuel sat up.

"Don't worry I'm ok, just his attack was very powerful," Samuel smiled. He stood up and yelled make me fly. Guess what, he flew. "Here's a disadvantage, if it can hear you it can her me," Samuel grinned. "Let me move five times faster than I can," Samuel yelled. Samuel rushed over to Sebastian. Sebastian blinked. Samuel grinned, "gah," Sebastian screamed. "Too late," Samuel smiled.

Sebastian flew into a moon rock. He got straight back up to his feet. He was filled with rage. His eyes started glowing. A bluish flame engulfed his hands.

"Ahhhh," Sebastian screamed. The bluish grew until his whole body was engulfed in it. "You won't beat me, AHH," Sebastian yelled. The bluish flame turned a reddish purple. The sky turned darker than it already was, Samuel and Lydia could feel his power and aura. They were terrified. His face twitched, sweat started running down his face. "Ahhh," Sebastian barked. He moved into a stance, he squatted with his arms at his waist. The flame grew. Electric sparks started appearing around him. His muscles doubled in size. He craned his head at Samuel and Emma like it took all his strength. "I'll give you ten seconds to run, although even if I give you a million you'd be dead in ten seconds," Sebastian laughed. Emma and Samuel looked at each other. They broke into a full speed run.

"AHHHHHHHHHHHHHH," Sebastian screamed. A huge beam of light surged out of his body. His eyes turned white. A large crater formed beneath him. Samuel looked back, he gasped. He was terrified. Sebastian's muscles shrunk. He was back to normal. But still there was a dark aura surrounding him. An energy blast materialized in his hand. Samuel and Emma were just little dots they were so far away. Sebastian transported to them. He appeared right before Samuel. Samuel almost slid into him.

"Ha," Sebastian smiled. He launched the energy blast. Samuel started running in the other direction. But he was too slow the blast got him. He was yet again down. He struggled to get up but he was too weak. Lydia went up to attack him but all he had to do was lift a finger and a surge of wind knocked her away. She got up. I guess I'll try to do the same thing Samuel did, she thought.

"Make me twice as powerful as Sebastian." She rushed at Sebastian. He was unable to track her speed. Before he knew it she kneed his face. He flew towards the ground. Samuel got up. He looked up in the air. Sebastian and Lydia were fighting once more. Lydia was faster than Sebastian but not as powerful. He knocked her to the ground with every blow.

"Let me be healed," Samuel yelled. He was back to full health.

"You arrogant little fiends," Sebastian moaned. "I'll have to dispose of you at once." Samuel frowned, he knew something bad was about to happen. A huge energy blast formed above his head. All the people of the Earth looked up in wonder. They could all see the huge bomb detonating. From Hungary to Tokyo, from Peru to China, the blast was half the size of the moon. "Ahhh," Sebastian screamed for possibly the final time.

"I wish Lydia was transported back to Earth," Samuel yelled.

"You know this will blow up the entire moon, ALL OF IT."

"Yes, but I'll be safe back home while you will take the blast dead on," Sebastian grinned.

"I won't let you, Sebastian!"

"Ha-ha-ha, goodbye, not just you Samuel but the moon as well," Sebastian laughed. The giant sized energy blast came down on Samuel. "I wish I was back home, now Samuel no more wishing because I won't be here neither will the mask. "Humph," Sebastian gasped. He was safe back. Sitting in his chair at his home witch was the prime minister's bedroom. "Ah, it's good to be home," Sebastian said relieved.

Samuel put his hands on the blast. Immediately he felt its great power. Already he was sinking into the ground. Already his quest was over. Already he let every one down. Already he was dying. His life flashed before his eyes all the good times and bad times. He put a positive smile on and let go. The explosion was massive. Lydia looked up. She saw the moon explode. She knew it was over. Samuel was over. Her quest was finished. But she wasn't sure Sebastian was. Even though. She was practically drowning in tears she marcher her way over to Sebastian's palace. She looked up nothing was left, and at that moment every one seemed to know who Sebastian really was. Sebastian Woods, the prisoner. All the way back in North Yorkshire her mom knew too, and she started making her way to London. She opened the main doors of his palace.

She was beat up but confident. Her eyes darted left to right looking for Sebastian. As she continued down the path, all of London's people marched in.

They were all angry. Maybe Sebastian could beat two people but not 8,300,000 people. The people barged into the room. Sebastian craned his head over at the people. For a split second he looked shocked at how many people there were. Then the wicked grin returned to his face.

"Back already, Emma," Sebastian cackled.

CHAPTER 7

A Final Wish

"Rah a giant flame ball shot from Sebastian's hands. All the people of London fled, screaming in terror most people left they had no idea how much power Sebastian had. But Lydia and only a few others stayed.

"Sebastian, give me the mask," Lydia yelled.

"Are you serious, you expect me to just give you the mask," Sebastian barked.

"No, I don't, but it's worth trying," Lydia said.

"You arrogant little runt, you should've died with your friend."

Lydia heard a whining voice in the background.

"Lydia finally I've found you, I can't believe you left like that, one second you're here the next you in London, you're so grounded when you get back to the…"

"Shut your flapping mouth," Lydia yelled.

"No I won't, your coming back to the house right now, before you're grounded for life," Lydia's mother whined.

"Just one final wish," Lydia asked.

"Your still talk about that stupid mask, gah, where is the thing,"Lydia's mother complained.

"Right here Madame," Sebastian grinned. He held up the mask.

"I'll rip it a part," Lydia's mother barked.

"I wish Samuel was back to life," Lydia screamed. Nothing happened.

"I told you, the magic is not real," Lydia's mother said confidently.

"But it is," Sebastian smiled. He mumbled something. Then a glass of wine appeared in his hand.

"I'll still rip it," Lydia's mother screamed.

"Why are you so annoying," Sebastian yelled.

"You should be nicer, and I'm not as annoying as this one right here, now that's annoying." She pointed at Lydia.

"No you're more annoying and now you're gone," Sebastian grinned. He picked her up and heaved her out of the building. Then he powered up, an immense light surged upward and went through the ceiling. Lydia backed up. He was more powerful than ever. The light faded, a mysterious figure dropped from the ceiling.

Sebastian put the mask on a table. Lydia's eyes stayed on the figure.

"What are you looking at, there's no one there," Sebastian yelled. He looked behind him.

Of course a person was standing near the table with the mask in his hands. He ripped he mask in two, Sebastian turned back to normal.

"No, what've you done," Sebastian cried.

"Well I ripped a mask," the figure smiled.

"Wait Samuel, is that you," Lydia questioned.

"Yes and I'll tell you how later," Samuel said grimly.

"But this is not over, Sebastian is still alive."

Sebastian looked around rapidly. He started running for the exit. As soon as he took one step out of the building.

"Now," Samuel yelled. A trap sprung up from the ground. Sebastian was hanging upside down by a foot and five police men were aiming guns at his head.

"Very well then, you caught me, now shoot me, or are you to scared," Sebastian grinned.

"No were not but we actually have mercy, so we'll let you live for a while longer," A police man said.

"Take him away," another chimed in. A police man knocked him out by hitting Sebastian hard in his skull with the handle of an AK74. Then the men slowly hoisted him down and started to drag him towards the nearest extremely high guarded penitentiary. Which was only five miles away the prison was called XX Doomed.

The police men heaved Sebastian into one of the six police cars with a loud thud. Before anyone of the Earth knew it all of their problems rode off into Sunday's brand new horizon. Everyone was relieved that a new day would be starting up. It was almost a party without words, Sebastian was finally finished. Lydia looked around. It was just her in the palace. Samuel wasn't there, but she heard a slight moaning coming from outside the palace. Lydia looked out of the empty doorway with disgust. Her mother was started to wake up from her slightly unconscious state.

She mumbled something like "Lydia be a dear and help me up". Lydia turned away not just because she couldn't understand her mother choppy and shaken voice but because she couldn't believe that she had not seen her in weeks and the first she says is "you're grounded for life young lady", and with that she walked out of the doorway barely looking at her mother and continued walking down a narrow backstreet of London.

"That's no way to treat your mother, you know you did do a terrible thing," Samuel whispered.

She looked behind her with a grave expression. It was hard to keep it though. Sooner or later she smiled. She helped her mom up still angry at her.

"Look on the bright side Lydia, you're alive, and Sebastian's gone don't be vexed," Samuel said cheerfully.

"At least ninety people were killed by that freak though," Lydia frowned.

"You can still wish upon this mask," Samuel smiled.

"But it didn't work for Sebastian why would it work for me," Lydia questioned.

"Sebastian never wished though, it still hasn't gone through a chemical change yet so it still has its magic," Samuel grinned.

"Oh I see, well then, I wish all the people injured or killed by Samuel returned to their normal state," Lydia yelled. The heavy feeling in the air was relieved. Lydia blinked. There were about one hundred people that had come back to life after her lively wish.

EPILOGUE

"You see Emma," Samuel chuckled. "You sleep talk and you talked about the mask and how you could stop him. How am alive is because your wish did become true, I just didn't how do you say spawn in the village, in fact I had no idea were I even was, until Sebastian's huge light beam gave it away, I was in the back streets of London not even ten minutes away," he explained.

"Oh wow I should've thought of that," Lydia grinned.

"Also I could still wish for anything I want, apparently you have to burn it to stop its magic, so let's get on with it," Samuel smiled.

Meanwhile

A teenage boy sat up from his ripped dirty recliner. He looked around angrily. He was dressed in ripped black shorts a plaid t-shirt and a musty red Yankees baseball cap. He was watching everything that happened off of his 32 inch television.

"Gah," he yelled. "Why do the good guys always win every time?" "Mother are you done with my chicken sandwich yet, I've been waiting for an hour," he barked.

A tall filthy woman stepped out from what must've been the kitchen. "It's j-just about ready d-dear," his mother trembled. "Not ready, I've had enough," He screamed. He picked up an old dirty book from under his recliner. His mother trembled with fear at the sight of it.

"Please son have mercy on me, I-I it just burnt a-and I h-had to re make it, p-please, no I-I'm begging you, no p-please," she screamed.

He flipped through a couple of pages then a smug look came to his face. He got in a strange stance, "Hadda ca tah," the boy yelled. Electric

64

bubbles spurred out of his hand, the surrounded his mother. "Goodbye," the boy grinned. The electric bubbles popped.

For a minute his mother stood there frozen staring practically through the boy. Then the boy clenched his hand. His mother disappeared with a cloud of smoke.

"Grr, ah," the boy screamed at the top of his lungs. His TV imploded, glass shattered, electric sparks flew from his body, "Now to complete the spell, Something living for something dead, except my giving and grant my wish," he chanted. A look-a-like tornado dug through his roof into his house. A small figure appeared within the eye of the tornado. The tornado thinned to reveal a small item, the mask, the mask of Legend. "Ha-ha-ha, I am Lucifer Child, and watch out Samuel and Lydia, I'm coming for you."

The End

Printed in the United States
By Bookmasters